Phonics

Ash and the Big Bad Fox

Sue Graves

W
FRANKLIN WATTS
LONDON • SYDNEY

First published in 2011 by
Franklin Watts
338 Euston Road
London NW1 3BH

Franklin Watts Australia
Level 17/207 Kent Street
Sydney NSW 2000

A CIP catalogue record for this book is available from the British Library.

ISBN: 978 1 4451 0427 0 (hbk)
ISBN: 978 1 4451 0440 9 (pbk)

Illustrations by Artful Doodlers Ltd.
Art Director: Jonathan Hair
Series Editor: Jackie Hamley
Series Designer: Matthew Lilly

Printed in China

Franklin Watts is a division of
Hachette Children's Books,
an Hachette UK company.

www.hachette.co.uk

Level 1 50 words
Concentrating on CVC words plus and, the, to

Level 2 70 words
Concentrating on double letter sounds and new letter sounds (ck, ff, ll, ss, j, v, w, x, y, z, zz) plus no, go, I

Level 3 100 words
Concentrating on new graphemes (qu, ch, sh, th, ng, ai, ee, igh, oa, oo, ar, or, ur, ow, oi, ear, air, ure, er) plus he, she, we, me, be, was, my, you, they, her, all

Level 4 150 words
Concentrating on adjacent consonants (CVCC/CCVC words) plus said, so, have, like, some, come, were, there, little, one, do, when, out, what

Polly and Kim
had a den.

The den was
in the woods.

Ash ran up.

Polly and Kim
hid in the den.

They saw a fox's ears.
The ears had lots of
fur on them.

They saw a fox's tail.
The tail had lots
of fur on it.

Polly and Kim
ran and hid.

Then they saw Ash!
Ash had fur ears.
And he had a fur tail.

It was not a big, bad fox at all.
It was a big, bad Ash!

Puzzles

Match the words that rhyme to the pictures!

hood

fear

tail

mail

her

ear

hear

rail

wood

sail

stood

fur

tear

23

Answers

tail – mail, rail, sail **wood** – hood, stood

ear – fear, hear, tear **fur** – her

Espresso Connections

This book may be used in conjunction with the Literacy area on Espresso to secure children's phonics learning. Here are some suggestions.

Word Machine
Encourage children to play the Word Machine Level 1. Demonstrate how the machine works, and then move on to the activities.

Ask children to find the correct first letter.
Then ask children to find the correct last letter.
Then ask children to find the correct middle letter.

Check that children are able to hear the difference between the letter sounds as different words come up.

Praise plausible attempts, such as substituting the letter "k" for "c" when attempting to find the hard c sound.

Finally, ask children to find all the letters of the word.

Spot the Word
Load a big book, for example **"Ash and his Family"** to play Spot the Word.

Give children pieces of paper with the high frequency words me or he or she or my. (The class could be split, with groups of children looking for different words.)

Ask children to note down on the paper each time they have seen or heard the word they are looking for.

At the end of the book, children should count up how many times their target word has been used. If their word has not been used, where could it be used?

Go back through the book together and see whether they got it right.

Praise plausible attempts, for example "her" for "he" and take the opportunity to point out why these words are different.